P9-EJZ-109

Books by Norma Simon

All Kinds of Families
Cats Do, Dogs Don't
Children Do, Grownups Don't
How Do I Feel?
I Am Not a Crybaby!
I Know What I Like
I'm Busy, Too
I Was So Mad!
I Wish I Had My Father
Mama Cat's Year
Nobody's Perfect, Not Even My Mother
Oh, That Cat!
The Saddest Time
Wedding Days
What Do I Do? *(English/Spanish)*
What Do I Say? *(English/Spanish)*
Where Does My Cat Sleep?
Why Am I Different?

I Was So Mad!

By NORMA SIMON

Illustrations by
DORA LEDER

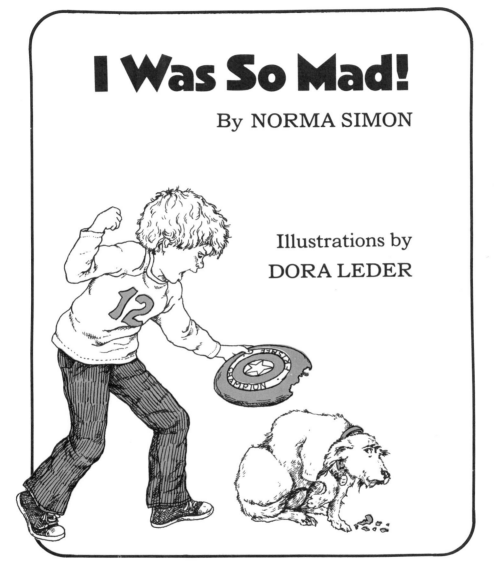

ALBERT WHITMAN & COMPANY
Morton Grove, Illinois

For Ed, Steffi, Wendy, and Jon, with thanks—N.S.

Library of Congress Cataloging-in-Publication Data

Simon, Norma.
  I was so mad!

    Summary: Text and pictures relate situations
which sometimes result in such reactions as frustration,
anxiety, humiliation, and loss of control.
    1. Anger—Juvenile literature. [1. Emotions]
I. Leder, Dora, illus. II. Title.
BF723.A4S55   152.4'2   73-22425
ISBN 0-8075-3520-6 lib. bdg.   0-8075-3519-2 pbk.

A Note About This Book

Suppose a child tells you something that obviously means a great deal. You listen and then ask, "How does that make you feel?" For as you help a child grow in ability to express feelings you also encourage growth in self-understanding of feelings.

Most of us struggle all our lives to understand and control a multitude of emotional responses. For the young child there are so many areas to master, motor coordination, perception, language, identity, relationships. And there is a wide range of deep and strong emotions which at times seems ready to engulf all else.

Healthy socialization and maturation include awareness and acceptance of one's own emotions and those of others. Some feelings, like love and loyalty, are readily acknowledged. But the emotions like anger, jealousy, and frustration may be repressed or ignored. This book's special value is in picturing situations that produce anger. It describes children's inner and outer struggles as they try to control their feelings and work them out in ways that are acceptable to themselves and others. Most girls and boys will find many situations familiar and respond to them.

There is in children a sense of outrage when they consider that their rights have not been respected or that these rights have been violated. It is good that children think of themselves as people, and as people with rights. When adults respond to this need for respect, then children learn to respect the rights of others. This book speaks to the adult as well as the child when it asks the adult to understand children's rights and feelings. It allows for acknowledgment even though behavior may not be approved. Feelings themselves are not denied, mocked, or rejected. It becomes possible to discuss why "I was so mad!"

Norma Simon

I get mad sometimes.
Do you get mad?
What makes *you* mad?

I get mad
   when I try to tie my shoe,
   and I try to tie my shoe,
   the more I try
   the less it ties.

I give up.

I get sooooooo mad—

and my mother helps me.

I get mad
    when somebody makes my room a mess,
    and my mother says,
    "*You* clean up that mess."

It's not fair.

I get mad and I tell her so.
She says, "Make them help you next time."

I get mad when the boys say,
"You have to be the mother.
You stay home and take care of the children."

They make me sooooooo mad.

I can be a cowgirl or a policewoman,
and I say so, too.

I get mad
    when I work on a building all morning,
    and somebody comes along
    and kicks it down.
I don't care what's bothering him.
I just get real mad.
I feel like kicking him.

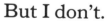

But I don't.

I get mad
    when the teacher says,
    "How do you know you don't like
    grape juice?
    Just try a little."

I *know* I don't like grape juice.
Why do I have to try it?

I just get mad.

I get mad
    when somebody says,
    "I bet you can't do *this* trick."
    And I know I can't,
    and I wish I could.

I just get mad
    and practice it when they're not around.

I get mad
    when I remember
    the time I wet my pants.
    Everybody teased me.
    It was awful.

I was mad at them all.
Didn't they ever have an accident?

I get mad
  when I'm not even tired
  and my mother calls,
  "REST TIME!"

Whether I want to or not
I have to take a rest.
I get sooooooo mad.

I'm too big for resting.

I get mad at my dog
   when he barks at kids on bikes.
   Barking really scares kids.
I yell at my dog
because I want him to be good.

I get mad at my cat
     when she runs across the road
     and I see a car coming.
I get so scared I spank her.

"Bad cat! You could be dead!" I say.

I get mad
    when I'm always the first one to come in.
    I hear everyone playing outside.
    I want to stay out as long as they do.

      I get mad—

It's one time I don't want to be first.

I get mad
    when my brother goes
    to the ballgame after supper
    and I have to go to bed.

I get mad.

I stay awake until he comes home,
and he tells me all about it.

I get mad
    when company comes
    to see the new baby.
    Fuss, fuss, fuss!
    Nobody talks to me.

What's so great about a baby?

I just get mad.

I get mad
  when it's supposed to be a swimming day
  and it gets cloudy and it pours.
Nobody's happy.

I get mad,

and I hop around in the rain in my bathing suit.

I get mad
  when the teacher picks on me.
  She blames me for something I didn't do.

That ever happen to you?
What do you do?

I get sooooooo mad,
but she believes me when I tell her
what happened.

I get mad
  when I write my name,
  and I know how it should look,
  but it looks wrong.

My father says writing isn't easy.

I just get mad.

I get mad
   when Grandma won't let me see
   my favorite TV show
   because I didn't eat all my dinner.
   She means it, too.

I get sooooooo mad.

(But most of the time I like her.)

I get mad
   when somebody breaks my best toy
   and doesn't even act sorry.

I want to cry.

I get so mad.
I wish I could break his toy.

I get mad
   at people who point fingers and tease me.
   I wish they'd go home.

I get sooooooo mad.

I *hate* to be teased.

My mother says
it's not bad to get mad.
Everybody gets mad — sometimes.

I'm not bad when I'm mad.
Some things just make you mad.

My father says
when he gets mad he feels
like a firecracker going off,
or a balloon popping,
    or a volcano exploding
        all over the place.

But it's not bad to get mad — sometimes.
        He sings a song about it —

There Was a Man and He Was Mad

Music Arranged by Janet Underhill

There was a man and he was mad,

He jumped in- to a pud-ding bag.

There was a man and he was mad,
He jumped into a pudding bag.

The pudding bag it was so fine,
He jumped into a bottle of wine.

The bottle of wine it was so thick,
He jumped onto a walking stick.

The walking stick it was so narrow,
He jumped into an old wheelbarrow.

The old wheelbarrow it was so rotten,
He jumped into a bag of cotton.

The bag of cotton it set on fire,
Blew him up to Jeremiah!

POUF! POUF! POUF!

Norma Simon

Because Norma Simon grew up reading voraciously and living vicariously through books she has a particular sensitivity to what books can mean to children. Her training in special fields of education and psychotherapy has alerted her to ways in which books can reassure children about their own emotions. In picture books such as *How Do I Feel?* and *I Know What I Like*, Mrs. Simon carefully shows a range of feelings. Being afraid as well as brave, feeling anxious as well as secure, angry as well as friendly—these are some of the emotions her books are about.

Like many persons who were born and grew up in a big city, in this case, New York, Norma Simon enjoys a home in a far less hectic environment. She and her family live on Cape Cod, where she not only writes but volunteers by teaching creative writing at an elementary school. She studied as an undergraduate at Brooklyn College, has done graduate work at the New School for Social Research, and holds a master's degree from Bank Street College. She has been writing since 1954 and has more than forty books to her credit. She is also a member of the Authors Guild.

Dora Leder

Dora Leder, who grew up in Budapest, cannot recall a time when she did not want to be an artist. She came to the United States when she was seventeen, and her career here commenced with professional training at an art school in Philadelphia.

Mrs. Leder lives in Pennsylvania with her husband, who is a designer, and her daughter, who is a photographer. This is the eighth book by Norma Simon that Mrs. Leder has illustrated, and she has illustrated several other children's books as well.